This book was created in Florence, Oregon.
We celebrate creativity and industry with the
Florence Festival of Books, September 28th, 2013.

Author: Gerald Duane "Boomer" Wright

Illustrated by: Tricia & Michael McHugh

Published by : Just Wright Books llc. © 2013 Just Wright Books LLC
Design, illustration, typesetting, editing by Tricia & Michael McHugh, JWB
Additional proofing and editing by Susan Wright.

This book was created, written, designed, illustrated and printed in the State of Oregon,
in the United States of America. All rights reserved, worldwide copyright 2013.

ISBN 978-0-615-87387-9   First Edition   2013

Sometimes you don't have to go very far; you just have to imagine.

Dedicated to our grandchildren:

Cartier, Caleb, Gabe, Ellie, Jovey and Dax.

We love you all with all our heart!

Papa Boomer & Grandma Susie

To Susan, my wonderful bride. Thank you for the support, advice, encouragement, ideas, and your unbending faith in God and a crazy guy that happens to be your husband. I love you!

This is Stella. I watched her being born in real life on June 2nd, 2012 at Sea Lion Caves. She was the inspiration for this story.

Being born on a rock ledge, just a few feet from the pounding Pacific Ocean, surrounded by hundreds of Steller sea lions, is not for the faint of heart.

However, a sea lion pup doesn't have much choice where it is born.

It was a cold and grey June morning at Sea Lion Caves, America's largest sea cave, where Stella's mother brought her suddenly into the world.

This is a story of how Stella the baby sea lion came to find "Boomer's Pond". It was inspired by real life observations of Steller sea lions at Sea Lion Caves.

For the first few months, Stella stayed close to her mother to nurse and for protection. The most dangerous time for Stella was when she left to find food. During those times, Stella would hide among the rocks or crawl next to another sleeping sea lion, so she would not easily be trampled by the huge bulls fighting each other, or the other sea lions moving around the rock ledge.

The bulls, built much like a bear, can grow to be 12 feet long and weigh up to about 2,000 pounds. Females, called cows, can reach 600 pounds and about 8 feet long.

Stella was always glad when her mother returned. They would call to each other with their own special barks. She would then nurse and fall asleep safe by her mother's side.

Through sun, wind, rain and surf, Stella grew little by little until her mother thought she was strong enough to go for her first swim.

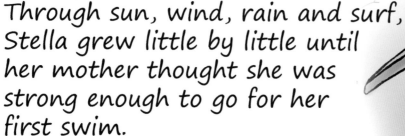

Stella's mother picked a fairly calm day with small surf and high tide, so it would be easy for Stella to get back on the rock ledge.

Stella was scared at first, but with gentle urging from her mother she took her first dive, well more like a belly flop actually.

After a quick swim, Stella's mother herded her back to the rock ledge where Stella used her flipper claws to climb out of the ocean water.

Stella loved to swim!

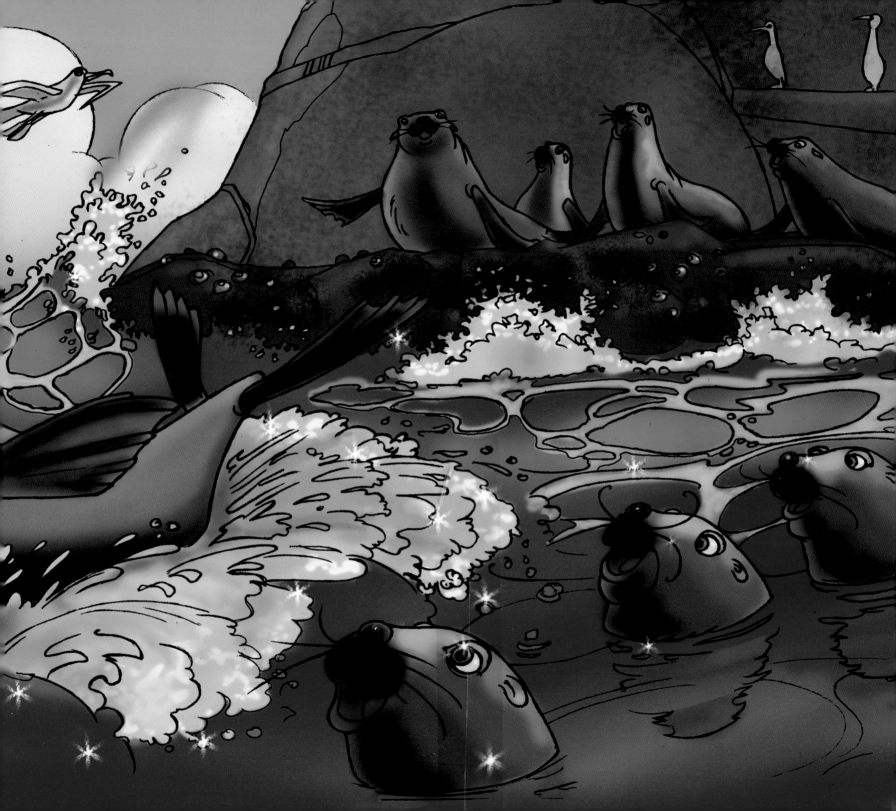

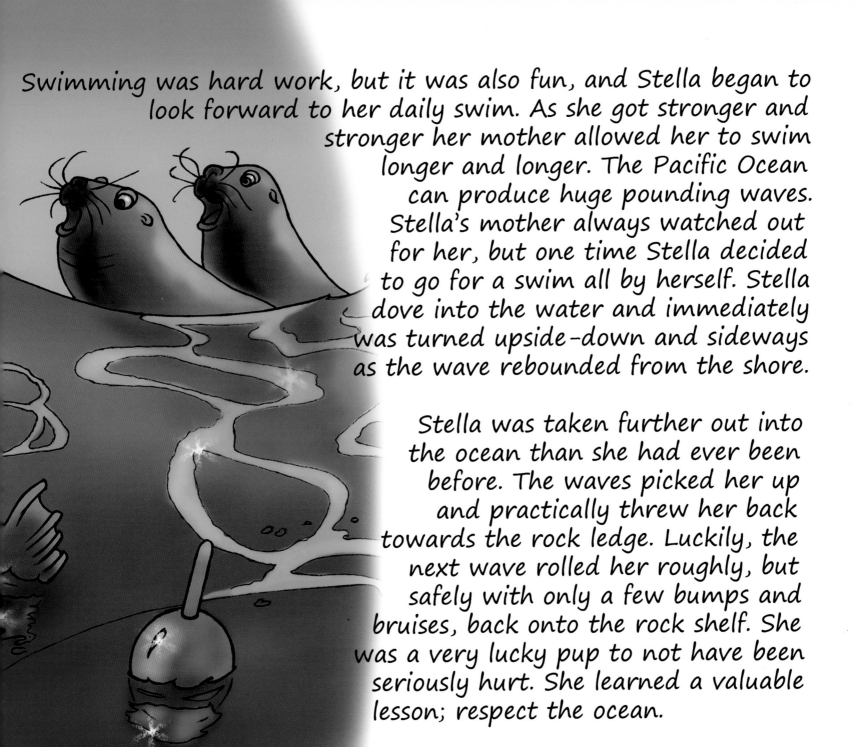

Swimming was hard work, but it was also fun, and Stella began to look forward to her daily swim. As she got stronger and stronger her mother allowed her to swim longer and longer. The Pacific Ocean can produce huge pounding waves. Stella's mother always watched out for her, but one time Stella decided to go for a swim all by herself. Stella dove into the water and immediately was turned upside-down and sideways as the wave rebounded from the shore.

Stella was taken further out into the ocean than she had ever been before. The waves picked her up and practically threw her back towards the rock ledge. Luckily, the next wave rolled her roughly, but safely with only a few bumps and bruises, back onto the rock shelf. She was a very lucky pup to not have been seriously hurt. She learned a valuable lesson; respect the ocean.

Spring turned to summer and summer turned to fall. Breeding season ended, and the bulls left the rock ledge to feed for the first time in months. The bulls never leave their territory during breeding season, even to feed. With the bulls gone it was less chaotic at the rock ledge, and much safer and easier to get around.

Her mother indicated to Stella that it was time to move from the rock ledge to another feeding ground up the coast.

On the way to her new home, her mother showed Stella how to dive to the shallow ocean bottom and look for food.

Stella would still be nursing for the next year. This was good practice for the time she would be weaned from her mother.

She found crab, sculpin, flounder, starfish, sea urchin, scallops, halibut, skates, clams and rockfish.

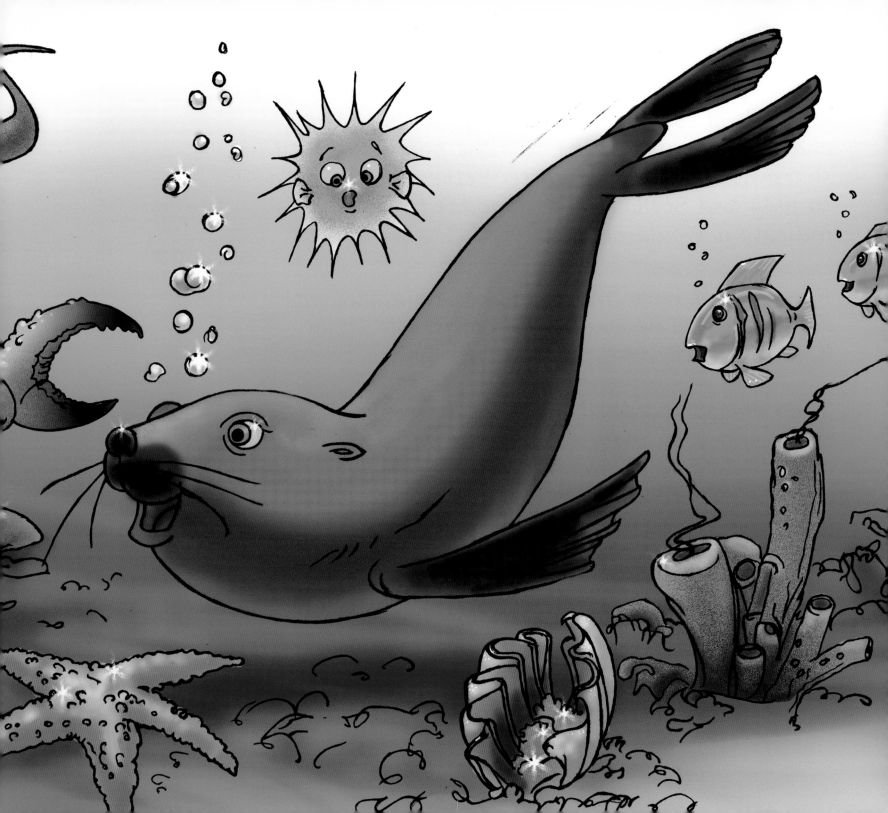

While swimming, Stella found the ocean was alive with all kinds of sea animals. Nearby, Stella heard a chattering sound, and Peter the porpoise poked his sharp nose out of the water. Peter invited Stella to play and Stella's mother nodded her head to indicate it would be okay.

Peter didn't have fins quite like Stella, but with his strong tail he could swim very fast. Stella had a hard time keeping up with him.

They played tag until they found a crab pot float, and then played catch-the-float for quite awhile. Next, Peter showed Stella how to surf on top of the waves. What fun they had! With the sun setting, Peter said goodbye to Stella and said he hoped they would get to play together another day, then Peter swam off. Stella and her mother swam to shore, climbed up on the rock ledge, and fell quickly asleep.

As they moved out into the ocean, she heard a "whoosh" and they saw a spray of water jet into the air. Then she saw the big "whoosh" and asked her mother what was happening.

Stella's mother told her there was a mother gray whale and her calf feeding nearby. She told her that gray whales were not dangerous, just very large. The mother whale can grow to be 50 feet long and weigh 35 tons. When the calf is born it is 12 feet long and weighs over a ton. They are not dangerous to sea lions. They use their bottom jaw to scoop up the sand from the ocean floor and sift small animals through their hair-like teeth, called baleen. Stella sensed her mother was nervous.

The mother gray whale had mentioned there were other whales in the area that were not as friendly as they were, and to be on guard. Stella didn't understand what that meant, but she understood she needed to be watchful.

The morning passed with more surfing, diving to the ocean bottom to have fun with the starfish, playing with other sea lion pups, floating on the surface in the sunshine, and taking a nap on shore. After her nap, off in the distance Stella noticed what she thought was a small spotted sea lion swimming near shore.

She swam over to introduce herslf and met Harry the harbor seal. Stella saw some differences between Harry and herself. First, Harry did not have outside earflaps like Stella. Harry's were just sort of like holes on the sides of his head.

Next, Stella noticed Harry's back flippers were not able to move like hers and were hairy, where Stella's were not. Where she could walk on all four flippers, Harry could only waddle like a duck on shore, as his rear flippers were not able to turn forward.

He was also much smaller than adult sea lions and had spots on his coat. He was very nice and polite to Stella, and after they had talked, Harry wished her well on their journey to their new home.

The ocean was calm making it easy to swim as they continued their journey to their new home. A sea gull would fly by once in a while, along with cormorants, puffins, pigeon guillemonts, and one pesky pelican in particular.

Patricia the pelican, who lived close to "Boomer's Pond", loved to tease the sea lions playing keep-a-way. She would open her big pouch of a beak, drop a herring in front of Stella and when she swam to get it, Patricia would dive in the water and scoop it up first with her huge beak.

Patricia thought this game was very funny, but Stella was soon having second thoughts, along with the poor little herring who was not sure if he was coming or going.

Then Patricia would chuckle and laugh at the frustrated sea lion pup and do it all again. After several times, Stella just decided to ignore her and she finally flew away to give some other sea lion a good teasing.

As evening came on, they finally arrived at their new pullout home. Stella was tired, and glad to have finally arrived.

She had learned a lot and met many new friends on the way.

Their new pullout home was near the Heceta Head Lighthouse, and a tired little sea lion pup quickly climbed up on the rocks and fell asleep.

She had been asleep only a few minutes when there arose a barking with her mother grabbing her by the nape of her neck. All the sea lions began moving from the water onto the rock ledge, and then moving as far back on the ledge as possible. She was dragged back from the edge. Once there, she peered over her mother to discover several large, 6 foot tall black fins sailing in the water. Her mother was terrified and told her the large black and white animals were orcas and enemies of the sea lions. They are one of the fastest ocean mammals and can out swim any sea lion. They are very dangerous. Stella's mother warned her that if she should see or hear a killer whale, she should swim to shore as fast as she can. Mother orca whales or killer whales, can grow to 23 feet long and weigh over 4 tons. Males can be much bigger than that. Fortunately, the orcas did not stay long.

The fall arrived quickly, and Stella grew to be strong and healthy under the sweeping lighthouse light. Between the lighthouse and the pullout was a small beach where the sea lions could sun themselves. Running along one end of the beach closest to the pullout was a swift creek flowing into the ocean. Stella had wanted to swim up the creek, but the water had been too low during the summer months. Now with the fall in full swing, the trees changing colors, and the rains returning, the creek was running deep and fast.

One afternoon, Stella and her mother decided to swim up the creek as they had heard that a large pond had been created behind a huge beaver dam. Stella had never seen a beaver before, much less a beaver dam, and was curious about seeing it. Although the creek was running fast, they had little trouble swimming up stream. After a few corners and some fast swimming, suddenly in front of them was a huge wall of mud and sticks. It was a large dam with a pond behind it covering about 3 acres.

They watched quietly as the beaver worked cutting new trees for the dam. This must be "Boomer's Pond" they thought. We should come visit another time and explore the beautiful pond and have some adventures her mother said.

With the coming of winter, Stella and her mother returned to the large sea cave, the humans call Sea Lion Caves.

The cave had been the winter home of the Steller sea lions for as long as any sea lion could remember. Inside was the protection from the winter storms and other predators. There were stories told by old sea lions of long ago, when the first man arrived by boat, and was stranded in the cave for several days during a big storm. Since that time, man seems to have protected the sea lions in the cave. Even with man close by, it was a good place to spend the winter with lots of food available nearby. The center rock, which is normally surrounded by water, was always crowded with bigger sea lions fighting over territory.

It all seemed silly to Stella, so she and her mother would find a quiet rock and plan their adventures at the beautiful little pond they had discovered, "Boomer's Pond".

Coming soon, the further adventures of Stella, the Steller Sea Lion at Boomer's Pond.

Elli the Elegant
Chinese Egret

Boomer Beaver

Caleb Wolf

Dax the Mallard Duck

Carl Cougar

Cartier Andrea Red Fox

Jovey Michael the
Mischievous Mink

Gabe the almost
Great Blue Heron

Otto Owl

Buddy Bear

Critters from "Boomer's Pond"

After the construction of the beaver dam by Boomer and Susie Beaver, many, many animals moved there. The Boomer's Pond Series are stories and adventures of the animals who now call Boomer's Pond home.